WINDSONG

WINDSONG

LYNN HALL

CHARLES SCRIBNER'S SONS / NEW YORK
Maxwell Macmillan Canada Toronto
Maxwell Macmillan International
New York Oxford Singapore Sydney

Charles Scribner's Sons Books for Young Readers
Macmillan Publishing Company
866 Third Avenue, New York, NY 10022

Maxwell Macmillan Canada, Inc.
1200 Eglinton Avenue East, Suite 200
Don Mills, Ontario M3C 3N1

Macmillan Publishing Company is part of
the Maxwell Communication Group of Companies.
First edition 10 9 8 7 6 5 4 3 2 1
Printed in the United States of America
Library of Congress Cataloging-in-Publication Data
Hall, Lynn.
Windsong / Lynn Hall. — 1st ed. p. cm.
Summary: Growing up in a small Missouri town and feeling unloved at home, thirteen-year-old Marty is determined to find a way to keep a special greyhound puppy from the kennel where she works.
ISBN 0-684-19439-2
[1. Dogs—Fiction. 2. Family problems—Fiction.] I. Title.
PZ7.H1458Wi 1992 [Fic]—dc20 91-46075

WINDSONG

1

The night before Windsong's first trial, I lay awake all night feeling her fear. She was half a mile away, in the kennel with the rest of the pups, but when she was that scared she just purely broadcast it.

I was the only one she could broadcast to.

I don't know what it was between her and me, but it was there from the time she was born. I'd been holding newborn greyhounds over at Orland's since I was a little kid, and I'd always got a kick out of feeling their soft, warm bellies and tiny rat-toenails. But when Windsong was born last fall, and I picked her up, something happened.

She was pure white and only half the size of the other two pups in the litter. And she'd been crying since the minute she was born, crying like she was hurting somewhere.

"Might as well bucket that one," Orland had said.

But I wrapped my hands around her and held her up against my neck, and right away she got still. Orland thought she'd died, but no, she was pressing against me, feeling the rhythm of my pulse, maybe hearing my heart-beat. It was what she needed.

It was what I needed, too. I was in one of my bad times then, with my family, and to have some living thing need me that way just plain saved me.

I made Orland promise not to bucket her. I said if she died on her own that was one thing, but if he drowned her like he did with puppies that were born bad, I'd never work in his kennels again. Since I worked for nothing, it was a pretty good threat.

School was on, then, so I had to leave the puppy part of the time, but every minute I could, I was with her. I carried her against my bare skin, under my shirt, while I worked around the kennels. I sat in the nest and held my hand under her while she nursed. Her first few days it was the only way she'd nurse at all, me making a mattress out of my palm and holding her up to her dam.

When the pups were six weeks old, Orland gave them their first shots. I held each puppy on the worktable while he pinched up a roll of skin over their shoulders and punched in the needle. The first two puppies flinched a little, and fussed after I set them down because the vaccine made a stinging bump under their skin. But Windsong screamed.

She screamed in fear more than pain, and her fear went right into my head like she was talking to me in words.

"Wasting my vaccine on that one," Orland muttered. "She ain't never going to turn out."

Turn out to be a racing dog was what he meant.

Orland was a big, fat man. Lots of people didn't like

him because he was so fat; they made fun of him. But he always treated me okay. Sure, he got a lot of free labor out of me. I knew that. I wasn't stupid. But it was work I wanted to do because I loved the dogs, so between him and me the situation was accepted as fair. I couldn't have my own dog because of my brother's allergies; Orland couldn't afford to hire kennel help and was too fat and wheezy to do the work. It was a fair trade-off.

We stood side by side, looking down into the pen that held the three weanling puppies. The two males were dark-marked, good-looking puppies, twice the size of Windsong. She looked like a little ghost beside them. Although she was still mostly white, faint tracings of gray brindle-stripes were beginning to show on her face.

Orland said, "It was an inbreeding, you know. An accident."

I knew. The dam of the litter had been bred by her own sire, Prize Is Gold. Prize was a big, powerful dog who just plain threw himself at his gate till the latch broke and he got in with his daughter, Golden Earrings, when she was ready to breed. Orland was madder than blazes, because Earrings was supposed to have raced that season, and she was the fastest thing he had in the kennel. But it was nobody's fault but his own, for not having better latches.

I said, "What's so bad about inbreeding, anyhow? I mean, they're still purebred greyhounds, and both of the parents are good dogs. Good racers. So why is it so bad, them being related to each other?"

He knew I really wanted to learn dogs, so he took time to explain stuff like this when I asked.

"Because everything behind the dogs gets intensified. You take a litter from two dogs that aren't related to each other, and in a four-generation pedigree you've got thirty different dogs contributing traits, sire and dam, grandsires and granddams, and so on, all different dogs with different good and bad points. But if you breed, say, a brother and sister, then they have the same parents and it cuts in half the number of contributing ancestors. See?"

"I guess. But . . ."

"So what that means is that a pup from a close breeding has that much more chance that bad faults in the background are going to show up. It has to do with genes and dominants and recessives and all that. But what it boils down to is that from an inbreeding like this, where the parents are closely related to each other, you might get something outstanding in the puppies, or total disaster. Because all the good and bad traits behind the dogs are concentrated. See?"

I didn't really. I needed to study up on genetics, and I wanted to, but Orland wouldn't lend me those books yet. He kept saying they were over my head.

Windsong had quit crying and digging at her sore shoulders, and she waddled over to the pen gate where I was. I scooped her up and let her nestle in my neck. She whimpered once, lightly, and slept.

Orland looked down at her, and at me. "Damn, I wish your folks would let you have a dog. I'd sure give you that one. She ain't never going to turn out."

He'd said that before, and every time he said it, it broke my heart.

* * *

On the morning of Windsong's trial, I got caught in the family breakfast. When I was lucky I got out of the house with just a handful of eat-and-run food, but sometimes they made me eat with them.

We might have looked like the all-American small town Midwest family. I don't know. We were a mess, under the surface, or else I was a total misfit and the rest of them were okay. I couldn't tell.

My mom was very pretty, very soft-spoken and sweet, except when she talked to my dad and then her voice just went tinny, like she could hardly stand the man. She had dark, soft hair that she wore long and kind of tied in at her neck, like an old-fashioned girl. I know for a fact that she was wild when she was young, and she was either trying to hide it or make up for it now. I'd heard from a couple of people around town that her parents more or less made her get married young, to steady, reliable Daddy, out of fear that her wildness would cause embarrassment to their family.

My daddy was a nice-looking man, square built, square faced, thick, wavy, reddish brown hair and good, strong features. He was such a quiet man, you had to be around him a good long time before you realized that the reason he never spoke out was that he never had a thought in his head. I know that's a disrespectful thing for a thirteen-year-old girl to say about her father, but it's true, anyhow.

I don't even know how to describe my brother, Matthew, I hate him so much. He's eighteen months younger than I; he looks like a carbon copy of Daddy; he is the child they both adore; and he is the reason I can't have the one thing I want more than anything in life. Want and need.

They made me sit down at the table and eat my toast and sliced bananas and drink my V-8, but they never once asked me what my day held. It was a crucial day in my life, but they didn't know or care, and if I'd tried to tell them, they still wouldn't have known or cared. Mom's mind was already on her job at the Divine Word Book and Bible Store. Daddy and Matt were going off together trying to sell Fast-Gro. And they were actually excited about it.

Fast-Gro was a sore point between Daddy and me. It was his wonderful invention that he figured on getting rich off, and I refused to help, so he turned that against me.

Daddy ran the feed mill. It was a junky old place at the edge of town. I hated it. When Grampa was alive, it was fun to go down there and have all the farmers poke their fingers at me and say, "This your granddaughter, Bill? She's going to be a heartbreaker, ain't she? Look at them big brown eyes. Look at them dimples." I'd giggle and they'd hoist me up on the counter and give me salted peanuts in the shell, which Grampa always had sitting around in burlap bags.

Grampa loved me. Grampa thought I was something special and valuable. After he died and Daddy took over the business, I couldn't stand the place anymore. Daddy always had Matt with him, showing him off to the farmers, showing him what the levers did and how the grinders and hoppers worked. There was no point in my being there.

Then the last year or so, Daddy started working on his big idea. Fast-Gro. It wasn't exactly dog food; it was just little plastic bags of stuff that looked like sawdust but was mineral supplements, vitamins, things like that. According to Daddy, kennel owners could buy the cheapest dog food around, add Fast-Gro to it, have full nutrition, and still come out cheaper than buying expensive dog food.

His big plan was to sell Fast-Gro, plus the supercheap dog food he made at the mill, to big kennel owners like Orland and get rich. And what he wanted me to do was talk Orland into buying it. I wouldn't.

So family breakfasts were fast and silent.

As soon as I could, I got away.

My bike lived on the front porch, since we didn't have a garage. I bumped it down the steps, did a racing leg-over mount since it was a boy's bike, and pedaled as hard as I could down the road toward the kennel.

My town, which is Jackson Ridge, Missouri, is on Highway 76, south of Ava. That's about fifty miles due east of Springfield, in the Mark Twain National Forest. Seventy-six is a broken-edged old blacktop that winds along the valley floor. Jackson Ridge is two blocks of old falling-down stores along the highway, most of them empty, plus a few little side roads with tired-looking little old houses and weedy yards.

When we go in to Springfield to shop at the malls and at Sears and to have lunch at the Pizza Hut, it seems more like the real world than Jackson Ridge, because it's what life looks like on television.

But yet, I know Jackson Ridge is me. It's something wrong with me, I think. I should love malls and noise and cheap jewelry and pierced ears and clothes and all the rest of it. I don't, because it scares me. Even if I had the money to buy that stuff, it still wouldn't make me beautiful, or confident around boys. I'd be ridiculous in that world.

They say Jackson Ridge is on the edge now. Springfield is growing all the time, and more people are buying up country land around it, building homes, nice homes, not like our little junky places. They say another ten years and Jackson Ridge will be a bedroom community full of yuppie families who commute to the city. Lord, I hope I can adjust when the time comes, because this is where I mean to live, all my life, right here working with Orland and his dogs.

My bike bumped off our rock road onto the smooth blacktop for the last part of the ride. The smoothness was a relief, but the uphill pull was hard. Three more years till I could drive! I got off and walked when I got to Orland's lane, and left the bike partway up his hill. Not only was his lane horribly steep, with hairpin switchbacks, it was also solid shale that split off in stairsteps of ragged rock. Orland's pickup went through tires every six months.

Coming up over the rim, I stopped to catch my breath and enjoy, as I always did. This was my place. Not my family's house in town. This. This was mine.

It was a green oval clearing surrounded by woods of jackpine and pin oak. Orland never mowed anything, but for some reason his place grew soft, pillowy grass that looked pretty without mowing. It had weeds, sure, but they were all flowering kinds of weeds. Up here, even though it was right above the town and the highway, everything was quiet and breezy and close to the sky.

There was Orland's house, which was nothing. And

there were the kennels and all the pens and exercise yards for the dogs, and behind it all, in another little clearing just off the main one, was the training track.

There, on the training track, this morning, we would find out if Windsong was going to turn out.

2

She was standing upright against her gate, waiting for me. Every time I came she was standing that way. Orland said she'd get in position about five or ten minutes before I came in sight, every single time. I don't know if she could hear my bike on the rocks at the bottom of the lane or what, but I loved it.

She was nearly full grown now, her head as high as my waist. Standing upright against her fencing, she was the same height as me; we looked straight into each other's eyes. Her love and need for me burned in her black eyes.

She was still almost pure white, with just the faint shadings of gray markings on her face. Her body was soft muscled like a child's, and she was several inches smaller than she should have been at this age. Orland held out little hope for her as a runner, and I knew he was probably right. But my love and need for her was just as fierce as hers for me, and Orland knew it.

He met me by her gate and handed me her racing collar and muzzle. "Let's get going," he said. "You take her, I'll take Wally and Wonder. Get her muzzle on her here."

She hated the muzzle. It scared her. I'd been working with her for a month now, trying to get her to accept it, but she still hated it. Her brothers, Wallbanger and Wonderdog, were muzzled and eager to get going while I was still wrestling with Windsong's head.

Orland always named his litters alphabetically. This was his *W* litter. The next litter had all had *X* names, then *Y*, and so forth. He was on his third time through the alphabet. He'd let me choose a *W* name for Windsong. My mom thought I named her after the perfume, but I didn't. I got the name from a haiku we'd just learned in school. Well, I learned it because I loved it so much; we didn't have to learn it, but it was in the book. It went:

Need friends ever speak?
There's tea to taste and windsong
from the garden trees.

It was the most beautiful thing I ever read, not just the poem but the idea of having a friend who was so close, and loved me so much, that we didn't have to speak to understand each other. I guess that was what I wanted the puppy to be for me.

Finally she gave in about the muzzle and followed me across the grass toward the training track. It was an oval like a miniature horse-racing track, inside a high-wire fence. The track itself was about twelve feet wide, running between the outer fence and a steel rail, waist high. The track was made of sawdust several inches deep.

I'd had Windsong on the track lots of times through the spring, leading her around, getting her used to it, running with her chasing me, to try to give her a love for running. But never before today had we tried her in the starting boxes, or with the lure. Or with other dogs. If she had what it took, she'd run. If not . . .

Orland handed me the boys' leashes while he wheeled out the starting boxes. They were a line of six cagelike boxes on a low, wheeled base. They had doors front and rear, so the dogs could be led in from the back and closed in. Then when Orland hit a button at the end of the rack, the front doors popped up, a bell jangled, and the mechanical lure on the rail took off.

It looked like a rabbit and smelled like a rabbit. In fact, Orland sewed fresh rabbit hides over it every few months to keep it smelling exciting to the dogs. All it was was a metal knob-thing that stuck out from the rail at about head height for the dogs. They chased it, and that made the race. Orland controlled the speed of the lure, so it was always just in front of the fastest dogs.

"Put her in the second box," he told me. "We'll put one on each side of her, see how that works."

Wally and Wonder had been in the boxes before. They knew what it was all about. Wally fought for a few seconds, then gave in, and Wonderdog just walked in and got into crouch position on his own.

I had to talk Windsong into the box, ease her in, reassure her till even I was starting to lose patience with her. She was terrified of the box. She shook so hard I could hear her teeth chatter.

"Stand clear," Orland commanded. He'd had enough of her, too.

I stood back behind the boxes and held my breath.

He hit the button. The bell jangled; the doors flew up; the lure jolted away up the rail.

Wally and Wonder leaped from the boxes and streaked after the lure, snarling at each other through their muzzles.

Windsong crouched within the box, her eyes glazed with terror.

Orland just looked at me and shook his head.

"Let's try her again," I pleaded. "I think the bell scared her. I think she has sharper hearing than most dogs, and the bell probably just scared her. Can you turn off the bell?"

Wally and Wonder came past, crossed the finish line, and got chunks of rabbit pelt to chew on for their reward. The rabbit was fresh-killed, with meat still on the pelt, and we had to hold them way apart from each other when we took off the muzzles, or they'd have fought for each other's chunks.

Orland took them back to the kennel then, and brought out Golden Earrings, who was in serious training now for the July meets at St. Louis and Omaha. We put her in the inside box, next to Windsong, who seemed to relax in her dam's presence.

Once again the boxes were closed, the button pushed.

This time Windsong exploded from her box a few leaps behind her dam, followed her for several strides, then slowed and turned to come back to me.

I sat in the sawdust and let her walk into my arms. Orland concentrated on Earrings till she'd finished her run and been put away. Windsong stood against me, leaning into me while I wrapped my arms around her and hid against her neck, like she used to hide in mine when she was little.

"It's no use," Orland said, over us. "She's too nervy. We could train her from now till doomsday and she'd never be able to handle the noise, the crowds, the whole business of racing. Besides that, she's too small. She could never compete with big reachy bitches like Earrings. And she doesn't have the instinct for it. A dog either loves to race or it doesn't, and if it's not there you can't put it in 'em."

"I know."

I did know. I'd been around Orland's kennel long enough to know that. But Windsong was such a part of me, it was like her failure was me failing, too, and I couldn't stand much more of that.

I pulled off her muzzle and held her long, bony face against mine. The big question was coming at us now.

Orland swung the starting boxes out of the way and sat on the post that held the rail. He shook a cigarette out of the pack he carried in the sleeve of his T-shirt and lit up.

"I can't go on with her, Marty," he said as gently as he could. "You know the facts of life in a racing kennel."

"I know, but couldn't you keep her for a pet, or for a brood bitch?"

"No pets. No brood bitches that don't have what it takes to be winners themselves. I'm operating on about a zero profit margin as it is. My government disability check just about buys groceries and dog food. I'm lucky if I win one race out of twenty, and then it's usually the low-stakes races, a few hundred in prize money. Bad dogs cost as much to feed as good ones, and they don't win a dime on the tracks. Now if Earrings hadn't got bred that last time,

I could've won some fair-sized stakes with her in Mississippi over the winter, but that didn't work out. Now, it might turn out to be a blessing in disguise because that Wonderdog pup looks like a flyer. You remember me saying an inbreeding might produce something fantastic, or a total disaster."

I was feeling sicker and sicker. "Windsong is the total disaster, you mean?"

"Afraid so, as a racer."

"Then give her to me."

The words hung in the still air of the clearing.

Orland's round face looked down at me like a man-in-the-moon face, his eyes disappearing behind the fat of his cheeks.

"You know you can have her if you want her, Marty. I'd rather that than putting her down and having you hate me in the night. But what would you do with her? You can't take her home."

I couldn't keep the tears back then, but I didn't sob or make any noise. Windsong softly licked them away, and some of the hate eased with the licking, for it was hate that made me cry. I hated my brother for his allergies and the way he took pride in them. And more than that, I hated my mom and my daddy for making Matt their only loved child, the only one whose needs were important.

"I want to come live with you," I said finally, when I could talk.

"You know you can't."

"I know you keep telling me I can't, but I still don't understand why. You live here all alone. I could cook and keep house for you, and help in the kennel, and still go to my same school and everything. And I could have Windsong with me if I lived here. You'd let me keep her as my own pet, I know you would."

He sighed. "You can't live here because I'm a man and you're a little girl, and people would make something out of it that it ain't. And besides, your folks would never let you live away from home. They love you. You just don't always feel like they do, but they do."

I didn't answer. Windsong stretched out on the sawdust beside me, then rolled over on her back and hooked her paw through my arm, asking for a chest rub.

"But you'll give her to me?" I said finally.

"If you want her."

"Yes."

I had no idea in the world how I was going to get around the problem at home. But I had to, someway, or Windsong would be put down. I'd watched Orland do it before, to dogs that didn't turn out. He'd lead them out in the woods, put his revolver against their heads right behind the eyes, and . . .

I'd sooner he did it to me than to Windsong.

She was mine now. Part of me did dances of joy at that, not because it was a surprise but because it was the fulfillment of what had always been, pure and natural, between me and this dog. The part of me that wasn't dancing was flat up against the reality that no dog would be allowed in my parents' house, now or ever.

3

The fort was the only answer I could think of. I knew they'd never let Windsong come in the house, and we didn't have a garage, but there was the fort.

I stood in the backyard with Windy pressed hard against my leg. She was so scared she just shook against me, but her head was up and she was looking around like she was interested, as if she might get to liking it here.

It was a good backyard. Our house was nothing, just a square box with old blue paint on it and patched roof shingles, but the backyard was good. It was nice and deep, and ended against a steep woodsy hillside. If you could have fought through the brush and scrambled all the way up it, you'd come out somewhere near Orland's clearing.

Our street also went up an east-west slope. When they made the street, they carved out stairsteps for the building lots, so everybody's yard was level, but each one was about ten feet higher than the next. The embankments along the sides of the yards were too steep to mow, so through the years trees had grown on them. Now, all the backyards were like Orland's clearing, flat and green in the middle, woods all around the edges.

At the back of ours, right where the woods and the steep part began, Daddy and Matt and I had built a log fort a long time ago. It was mainly for Matt, I knew. He was too little to appreciate it then, but I wasn't. I loved the fort. I loved working with Daddy that summer, helping him. I thought if I scrambled all over that hillside finding the right trees for him to cut down and cut up, if I held while he pounded and brought him every tool he needed, and never whined or got tired of the project like Matt did, then in the end it would be my fort, too. When it was finished, he would say, "Now Matt and Martha, this is Fort Hogan, and it belongs to both of you. And Matt, you have to share with your sister."

But he never did. By the time it was finished Matt had lost all interest in it. He was only seven. And Daddy was tired and crabby and acted like he didn't care what happened to the darned fort. So I had it to myself for a few days, and then Matt moved in and took over, and I just let him have it. For a few years he and his friends used it for a clubhouse, where of course I was not allowed. Then he outgrew it, and nobody used it for anything anymore.

It was about five feet square, about four feet high, made of sapling logs standing upright, like old Indian forts in pictures. The roof was just a few logs laid across, with part of an old tent canvas over them. There was a doorway big enough for a kid to crawl through, but no windows. With all the cracks between the logs, windows weren't necessary.

I led Windy toward the fort and pushed open the door.

"It's okay, girl. You're going to live here. This'll be fine." I crawled in first, and she followed me.

It was fairly clean inside. There were some old junked toys of Matt's and some stuff from his club: candles and matches and strips of red cloth they'd used for some secret deal they had. I shoved everything over in one corner, then settled in to spend the afternoon with Windy in the fort, hoping she'd feel secure there by the time Mom and Daddy got home.

I was so jittered up I didn't know what to feel. Windy was mine now. That fact soared above everything else. From now on it was the peg I was hanging my life from. Just having Windy, taking care of her. Protecting her. She was so beautiful with her long, slim legs and tail and her deep, curved body and lean, nervous head. Just owning her made me more than I'd been before. It made me a genuine person. Myself. Not anyone's daughter or sister or kennel help. My own self.

Knowing that, I could never give her up, now that she was mine. And yet, it was very possible that they would make me give her up, and if they did, she would die.

I spent that endless afternoon curled on the dirt floor of the fort, with Windsong stretched against me. I stared out through the cracks at my parents' house and played over and over in my mind all that was about to happen.

At a little after five, Mom drove in.

"Okay, this is it, Windy. You have to stay here. I'll come back as soon as I can." Orland had given me an old braided rawhide leash to bring her home with. I tied it to the post at the edge of the door, kissed her, and crawled out to do battle for her.

When I came into the house Mom was on the phone, talking soft and hunching her shoulders around what she was doing. She'd been doing that lately, and then straightening up and getting a louder voice when she saw me.

"Yes, Brother, I'll surely do that. God bless you, too."

I tried not to let my shudder show. This was no time to get off on a fight about Brother George.

As Mom hung up, Windy started barking.

Mom's head spun around, following the sound. She looked at me.

"Lord, child, where have you been? You look like a coal miner. Get in there and wash, and don't wipe the dirt off on the towels, hear? What is that dog barking? Did Everlys get a dog?"

I held onto the back of a kitchen chair. "She's my dog. Windsong. Orland gave her to me."

She stared at me. "Gave her to you. Orland gave you a dog?"

I stood my ground.

"Well then you better give it right back to him, and you do it now. We'll wait supper."

"No ma'am. I can't give her back. She's mine. I love her. She didn't turn out, as a racer, and Orland can't afford to keep dogs that don't turn out, so it was either give her to me or shoot her. I love her, Mama." I fought my tears back.

All of a sudden Mom looked too tired to stand up. She pulled out a chair and sat, and so did I, hoping it was a good sign.

"You shouldn't have taken a dog, Marty. You know we can't have a dog here. You know Matt's allergic."

"But I love her. I *need* her, Mom. I have to have something in life that loves me. And Windy, Mom, ever since she was born she's only happy when she's with me. She used to cry all the time except when I'd carry her around in my shirt while I was cleaning pens. She's a real special dog. She can hear things none of the other dogs can hear, and she's always standing up on her hind legs looking out the gate, five minutes before I get there. None of the other dogs ever did anything like that. Windy and I belong to each other."

Mom sighed and leaned back in her chair and slipped off her shoes. The salty smell of sweaty feet came up to me.

"Honey, you know better than this. You're thirteen years old. You'd ought to know better than to get attached to a dog when you know you can't keep it. Now, best take it back to Orland's right now. I'll drive you over, if you want."

"I can't give her back," I wailed. "Mom, Orland will shoot her if I do. I love her. You can't make me have her killed. You can't!"

"I'm sorry, but I don't know what I can do about it, hon. We can't have Matt wheezing. You know how he gets. You can't expect your brother to suffer just so you can have a pet."

"But I have to suffer!" I clenched my jaws around the words. "All you guys ever think about is what Matt wants. You never pay any attention to what I want. I need this dog. Really badly. I *need* her, and she needs me. And I think it's my turn."

Daddy's pickup truck rattled in then and stopped beside

Mom's car. Windy barked again. I looked out the kitchen window and saw her standing half out the fort door, her head pulled low by the leash. I wanted to get back out to her.

Daddy and Matt came in. Anywhere Matt was, there was always noise. It was like he disturbed the air with electrical energy; things just crackled around him. He banged in through the door and said, loudly, "There's a dog in my fort."

"She's mine," I said, and gave him a hard look in the eye.

"Well get it out of my fort. You can't have a dog in my fort. You can't have a dog at all, Marty. I'm allergic."

He said it with the absolute calm of victory. He didn't need to yell or cry or even argue, to get everything he wanted. All he had to do was say the magic words.

Daddy came in then. "What's that dog doing in our yard?"

I turned the full strength of my willpower on him and explained again about Windy.

"We can't have a dog on the place, and that's final. You know your brother has . . ."

"Allergies," I snarled. "If I hear the word one more time . . ."

"Well, it's a fact, and you'd better face it." He turned toward Mom and said, "Haven't you started supper yet?"

She got that hard look on her face. "I'll start supper when we get this dog thing settled. Some things are more important than eating. You've got to admit Marty does have a point, Harold. She has had to give up things she's wanted, for Matt's sake. This dog is important to her, and she says Orland will shoot it if she takes it back."

"Ahh." Daddy dismissed the notion. "No point discussing it. What Orland does with his dogs is no skin off my nose, but we aren't having it here, and that's final."

"Not in the house," I said, "but why can't she live in the fort? I'd fix it up before winter so it would be warm enough, and I'd build a fence around it so she could move around and have exercise, and I'd do all the work. Why wouldn't that be okay?"

Matt said, "It's my fort. You can't have it."

"It should be more mine than yours," I said evenly. "I did more of the work of building it, and you had all the use of it for three years, you and your stupid club. And then you lost interest in it. You haven't been out there for the last year. Fair is fair. It's my turn now."

"Can't you at least be getting the potatoes started?" Daddy whined. "It's going on six, and you haven't even got the potatoes cooking."

Moving furiously, Mom tied her apron over her work dress and started whipping the potato peeler, sending little bits of peel flying all over the counter. Her stocking feet were planted wide, like she was mad.

I began to get the feeling she was going to fight for my side, if only to be fighting Daddy.

"Marty's right," she said, partway into her second potato. "Matt isn't using that old fort anymore. I say that if the dog stays out there and doesn't bother Matt's allergies, we ought to let her keep it."

Daddy didn't answer, but he walked, heavy and loud,

into the living room to watch the news. I wanted to ask him for some dog food from the mill for Windy, but I was afraid to. There were always spillages and ripped bags that couldn't be sold. It wouldn't cost Daddy a penny to let me have all the dog food Windy needed, if only he'd be willing. But I felt all that hate in the air between them, and I knew that, if Mom was taking my side as a way of fighting him, he was doing the same thing. Going against me and Windy as a way to hurt her.

I didn't know what was going on between them, only that it had been in the air the past seven, eight months. It began when Mom went to work at the Divine Word Book and Bible Store and started going to Brother George's services. But I didn't understand it.

Matt stomped off upstairs to his room. I went and stood beside Mom at the sink. "Want me to help?"

She was still whipping the peeler over the last of the potatoes, whittling them down to wasted nubs. If I'd wasted that much potato, she'd have yelled at me.

"No. You go take care of your dog. Get it some water. Use that old blue roaster if you want."

"She needs food," I said faintly.

"Back of the pickup."

I took Windy the roaster full of water, then scooped a pan full of Daddy's cheap dog food from a nearly empty bag in the back of his pickup. He'd been passing out samples of it with his Fast-Gro; he'd never miss it.

I stayed with Windy till Mom called supper. Windy didn't like the cheap food and wouldn't eat it, but she did drink lots of water. It was beginning to seem as though things might turn out perfect after all.

4

Jodie came over after supper. I called and told her about Windy, and she came over with the two things I needed most, a long rope and an old blanket her mom didn't want anymore.

Jodie was what I would have to call my best friend, not counting Orland. When school was on, we didn't spend much time together. She was a grade behind me, and we both had other kids we ran around with at school. But in the summer, she was closest. She lived down at the end of my block, and we were the only girls our age in the neighborhood, so that was why we were friends.

But she had a best friend besides me, her cousin Raye, and she was always rubbing it in, what her and Raye did together, stuff like that. She was letting me know that I needed her more than she needed me. I think maybe she did it because I was a year older and she had to even the score, but it made me feel bad anyhow. I'd go for days at a time not calling her or going over there, just to see if she'd call me, or come over to my house. Sometimes she did, sometimes not, depending on how much time she and Raye were spending together.

But the dog was big enough news for us to forget all that stuff and just get together. Jodie didn't like my working at Orland's all the time, because it shut her out. She'd never let me talk about the dogs, always changed the subject. Now, though, she seemed excited about having access to a genuine purebred racing greyhound.

Jodie was smaller than me, and blonder, and thinner faced. There are a lot of old-time families in this area that all look alike, as if they were from the same bloodlines. They had thin, pale hair and not much eyebrows or eyelashes, and little fading-away chins, and generally crowded, crooked teeth. We had an awful lot of kids like that at school, and most of them were at the bottom of the class. Mom said it was poor nutrition and not to make fun of them. Jodie was smart, though.

She could be mean as a snake sometimes, but nobody could say she was dumb.

"That's a funny-looking dog," she said when she got there. "How come it looks so stringed out?"

"She's a greyhound, stupid. They're bred that way so they can run faster than any other dog in the world. Look. See how deep and flat her body is? That's so she can cut a hole through the wind and still have room for great big lungs and heart. And see how her body curves up and then down again? That gives her like a hinge in the middle of her body, to make her strides that much longer. It's not just her legs reaching forward to take a stride; it's her whole body folding and extending on itself and adding to the length of her legs, so each stride is a giant leap."

Jodie looked at me, impressed.

Windy came forward on her prancy feet and stretched her nose to touch Jodie. Jodie stroked her head. Windy didn't wag her tail or respond, just accepted Jodie's hand and then came back to me, like a kid that did a good job shaking hands with company.

We fixed the blanket on the fort floor as a bed for her, and then we tied the long clothesline rope to her collar and let her range and romp around the yard, stretching her legs.

"What are you going to do with her?" Jodie asked after a while.

The dream hatched as I told it. "I'm going to get Orland to let me breed her to one of his studs and get puppies. I can sell some of them and make money, and I'll keep the best one and race it. Heck, by the time I'm out of high school, I could have my own string, working with Orland and keeping them at his kennel and traveling to the races with him."

"Would your folks let you?"

"No. I'd do it anyway, though. When I get out of school, they can't stop me."

"They'd have a fit. My folks would, if it was me. They want me to go to Oral Roberts University. Heck, I want you to go there, too, so I'll know somebody."

I laughed. No bible college for me. Dog racing, that was going to be my life. But I wasn't talking about it yet, to anybody except Orland and sometimes Jodie. I didn't want my folks telling me I had to stay away from Orland's kennels, and that's what they'd do if they thought I was this serious about it.

* * *

Jodie went home and I went in the house. It was dark by then, and the mosquitoes were all over me, turning red with my blood before I could hardly get my hand up to smash them.

Daddy and Matt were in the living room watching TV. Mom and the phone were both out of sight, the phone cord leading to the screen porch off the dining room. I could hear her voice, that almost-whisper voice that somehow scared me. I got myself a kool-cube from the freezer, and a paper towel to drip onto, and went into the living room.

Kool-cubes are Mom's cheap form of Popsicles, just ice cubes made of Kool-Aid, with toothpicks stuck in them. They tasted really good if you ate them fast enough to keep ahead of the melting, and they were so cheap we could have as many as we wanted.

I offered mine to Matt. He took it but acted like he begrudged me his effort to say thanks. I went back and got two more.

Looking at him across the dark living room, in just the blue television light, I could tell Matt was mad at me. I honestly didn't know why he should be. I wasn't taking a thing away from him, only fighting for what I wanted and needed for myself.

At the end of the program he got up and wandered out to the screen porch, hunting Mom. She was still on the phone.

"Go on now, I'm talking." Her voice sounded sharper than usual when she talked to Matt.

He came back red faced and furious looking.

"Want to play hangman or something?" I asked. Mostly I ignored his bad moods, but with Windy's future so iffy, and so important, I felt like I'd better make peace with him if I could.

"No. Stupid game."

I went over and sat on the floor beside him, where we could talk without keeping Daddy from hearing the TV. "Matt, don't get mad at me about the dog, will you? Please? I love her so much. And you really haven't been using the fort for a long time. You know that."

"I'm allergic," he muttered stubbornly.

"I know that. That's why I'm not trying to keep her in the house, where she'd make you wheeze. I'm willing to risk her health and welfare, come winter, making her stay out in a cold drafty place like that. I think you should meet me halfway and at least not begrudge her to me."

He didn't say anything.

Mom finally came in from the porch, carrying the phone and looking faraway. Matt jumped up and ran to her for a hug. I hadn't seen him do that in years. I just stared.

She gave him an absentminded pat and held him off away from her. I wanted to cheer. It was like a vote on my side.

"I've got to go back to the store for a little while," she said. "I got to thinking, I'm not sure I locked that back door when I went out. I'll be back. Maybe I'll run up to Ava and get some of that good chocolate-chip ice cream, okay?"

Daddy turned and stared hard at her, and said nothing.

Matt said, "I want to go with. I want to go with."

"No. I'll be right back."

"But I want to go with," he wailed. Big baby.

"Matthew, shut up! I said no. Can't I have any peace?"

He stared after her, mouth hanging. Never ever in our lives had she talked to him that way. To me once in a while, but never to Matt.

I wondered if maybe this dog thing was splitting us into two sides, me and Mom against Matt and Daddy.

Somewhere deep in my head, I wanted that. I wanted her to love me, to stand up for me against Matt.

The upstairs of our house was all one room. Matt had from the stairway, right, and I had from the stairway, left. The roof sloped in on all four sides, so there wasn't a lot of standing-up room, but each of us had one big dormer, where the wall went straight up to make room for windows. Those gave us some air and space anyhow.

The walls were plywood paneling nailed to the rafters. It bulged in lots of places where the wood had warped, but I didn't care. I pretended it was a kennel manager's apartment on a big estate, and I was in charge of all the beautiful dogs. My bed was up against the sloping wall-ceiling. Lots of times I could hear squirrels as plain as anything, scrabbling over the roof shingles not a foot from my head.

Luckily, my window was the one that faced the back-yard. I went to the window over and over in the night, to be sure Windsong was all right. The moon was bright enough to show me slivers of her whiteness through the poles of the fort. If I could have got away with it, I'd have slept out there with her that first night so she wouldn't be scared.

But she didn't seem to be scared. She'd settled right down and gone to sleep, even in that strange place, and I wasn't getting any mental fear-messages from her at all.

Maybe she was relieved to be away from the other dogs, and to know she wouldn't have to be a racer.

Something woke me, early in the morning. I lay there in bed listening, but everything was quiet and normal.

I got up and went downstairs to the bathroom and, coming up again, I saw that Matt's bed was empty.

I went to the window. No sign of him.

He never got up early when he didn't have to.

Something scared me, in the back of my mind.

I got on my shorts and shirt and went down again. Mom was just staggering out of the bathroom. She had no balance till she was clear awake.

"Where's Matt?" I asked her.

She just looked at me with bleary eyes and steadied herself along the kitchen counter to the coffee pot.

The door open, and Matt came in. My heart froze up.

He was wheezing, and red eyed, and fighting for breath.

Mom woke up fast then, and got him his pills and held his head while he swallowed, and steadied and soothed him until his breathing smoothed out and he could talk.

"Make her get rid of that dog," he said. "I can't stand it."

Mom looked at me, a long, regretful look, and I knew he had won.

"That's no fair," I wailed. "He must have been out there in the fort with her. He wouldn't be allergic if he'd leave her alone. That's not fair."

“I was not,” he said, his voice weak and coughy. “I was just in the backyard. If I can’t even be in my own backyard without almost dying . . .”

Fury rose in me. “You were not just in the backyard. I looked out the window and I never saw you, so you had to be in that fort. That’s the only place you could have been, and me not see you from the window. And if you were in the fort, it’s your own fault she made you wheeze, it’s not Windy’s. All you have to do is stay away from her and you’ll be fine. You did it on purpose! Mom, he did it on purpose. Don’t let him get away with it.”

But it was no good.

I watched in despair and disbelief as Mom’s face told me what she couldn’t quite say in words.

Matt had won.

Windy would have to go.

5

The only thing I could think of was Ushie.

Before Mom left for work she told me in a hard, sorry voice that I'd have to have Windy out of there today, before Matt and Daddy came home for supper. I'd sat most of the morning in the fort with Windy, going crazy in my head, until finally I thought of Ushie.

It was probably as bad as all my other ideas, but it was the only one I had.

Her name was Mrs. Ursula Fretty, but everyone called her Ushie. For a while, when I was ten, I took piano lessons from her. Back then I was still trying to do anything I could to get attention from Mom and Daddy. I had this big dream that I'd be such a good piano player that they'd come to my recitals and clap and hug me and tell me how proud they were of me. I had dreams of Mom going to work and bragging on me to everybody that came into the store, and the same with Daddy at the feed mill.

But it was a stupid idea. We didn't have a piano for me to practice on, so it took me forever to get my fingers trained. The other kids who took from Ushie were in Book

Three while I was still in Book One. Ushie kept telling me it wasn't my fault, that I was doing real well for not being able to practice between lessons. She even told me I could come and use her piano to practice on while she was having supper. But that was when we had supper at home, and I had to be there for that.

After a while I felt so bad about it that I wanted to quit the lessons. I started crying right there on the piano bench, and spilled my guts about everything, why I wanted to learn to play, so my folks would love me, and all that. Ushie came and sat beside me and let me cry on her, and she petted my hair and said, "There, there," and let me cry it out. I loved her so much.

Then she told me that the reason I wasn't learning well was that I was trying to cheat the music, trying to use it for dishonest reasons, and that if I had truly loved the piano for itself, I'd be learning and doing well, because I'd be willing to pay the price in practice time, somehow. She was right.

Then she said that I could quit if I wanted to, but that she'd sure miss me. Something about the way she said it made me think of something she hadn't said—that she needed the money from my lessons. She didn't have very many students, and there was a rumor around town that she sometimes bought canned dog food and ate it herself because it was cheaper than real food.

So we came to a sort of compromise deal. I kept coming at lesson time, and bringing my five dollars, but I didn't have lessons. Ushie and I would sit in her living room and talk, or she'd play some of her old German songs for me. Sometimes she played scratchy old records of Wagner operas; I'd never heard of them, but they were kind of exciting. She'd tell me the stories behind the music.

Mostly we just talked, though. She liked having someone listen while she remembered out loud. She had been a young girl in Germany during World War II, and she did what most of her friends were doing then, married an American serviceman as a way to get out of Germany and into this country. The boy she married brought her back to his hometown, Jackson Ridge, Missouri, dumped her on his mother's front porch, and took off, and she never saw him again.

That was fifty years ago. She'd been lonesome a very long time.

Daddy and Matt came home for lunch, so I stayed hidden in the fort with Windy till they took off again. In spite of all my worry about whether I could keep her alive, I was loving this time of being close to her. She'd stretch out on the ground, on her back, with her head in my lap and one delicate forepaw hooked over my wrist, and she'd just stare up into my eyes. She never got enough of it, and neither did I. It was like we both knew it couldn't last.

After Daddy and Matt drove off, I took Windy up to the back of the house and gave her a bath from the hose. I wanted to get the kennel smell off of her, and the stains on her back legs from the grass and dirt.

When she was sparkling white and tied out to dry, I got myself cleaned up and took the forty dollars of Christmas money I'd hidden behind one of the bulges in the wall paneling near my bed.

Windy and I walked across town. She was eager, spooky,

dancy. She had springs in her feet. I loved her so much.

Down the length of Main Street and up the block behind the old dead movie theater, and there was Ushie's house, last one on the block before the mountainside began.

It looked like it should be her house; it was brown and little and cute, with window boxes and flowers. It reminded me of a picture of houses in the Swiss Alps, in a book at school.

Ushie was sitting in the backyard, in a lawn chair, aiming the hose at her vegetable garden. She was short and fat and looked funny because she didn't match. Her face was covered with makeup, black eyebrows, rosy cheeks, orange skin down to the bottom of her neck, with her purplish red curly hair and a huge straw hat. Below that was a great big sleeveless shirt, like a tent, and below that were fat, white, bare legs with blue and purple veins all over them. Her feet were bare, too, and the toes twisted and lapped over each other.

She didn't hear me coming over the splash of the hose water on the potato leaves.

"Ushie," I yelled.

She jumped. "Marty. What a nice surprise." She turned off the hose and tucked her feet under the chair out of sight. "Where did you get the dog?"

I took Windy over to her. Windy reached out her nose and waved her tail gently. It was more than she'd done for Jodie last night.

"She's mine. Her name is Windsong. I named her myself."

"Ah. She's a greyhound, isn't she? They're a fine breed.

Very ancient, very noble. You are honored, to own one. I didn't know you were such a rich lady now."

I crossed my legs and sank to the grass in one neat movement. "Orland gave her to me. I been working for him, up at his kennel. I help him clean runs and stuff. She didn't turn out, as a racer, so he gave her to me. But my folks won't let me keep her because my brother is allergic."

Hatred rippled through my voice. Ushie looked down at me, startled.

"He can't help that, I'm sure."

"No, but he uses it to get whatever he wants and to keep me from getting anything I want. I had it all fixed up to keep Windy in this old play fort way at the back of our yard. She wasn't hurting anything back there. She was really good, last night. Never barked nor bothered anything. And you know what Matt did? He snuck out there real early this morning and crawled in with her and probably rubbed his face against her or something. 'Cause when he came in the house he was all wheezy and red eyed, and Mom . . ."

I started breaking down.

Ushie leaned forward and patted my arm.

"Mom won't let me keep Windy, even at the back of the yard, and if I take her back to Orland he's going to shoot her. He won't keep a dog that can't race. So I can't take her back there. I love her so much, Ushie."

"So you come to me, eh?"

Softly, fearfully, I said, "I want to come live with you. Me and Windy. Can we?"

"No." She seemed amused. "That would be against the

laws, you know. Your parents are your legal guardians till you're of age, and it would take an awful strong reason to change that. A dog, that's not enough of a reason, not for the law."

"But what if they didn't care? What if they wanted me to live over here with you? I don't think they'd care. Please? I have to be with Windy, and we could both live here with you, and keep you company, and help in your garden. It'd be neat."

"Neat for you, maybe. I'm too old for that kind of upsets in my life. Sometimes I can't hardly stand those kids that take lessons from me. Their noise. All that energy. I like you okay, Marty, you're nice and quiet, but I'm an old lady. I need my rest. And besides, your folks, they're good people. It would hurt them awful if you said you didn't want to live with them anymore. You can't hurt people like that, girl."

"They hurt me, all the time. They love Matt and not me."

"You're talking nonsense. They love you. I think you just demand proof of it all the time, and that don't always work."

I was silent. I felt angry, betrayed by the one person I was sure I could count on.

Ushie said, more kindly, "You want to give me that dog? I'll take the dog, if that's what you want."

My head came up, my hand clenched on Windy's collar. No! It wasn't what I wanted. I wanted her to take both of us, together. Not just Windy. She was mine!

But I kept silent. I didn't want to admit it, but it would

be a solution. It would mean Windy would live and have a good home and I could see her a lot.

But . . . I wept inside. She wouldn't be mine.

She might start loving Ushie as much as me.

I couldn't stand that.

After a while I stood up and, slowly, held out my Christmas money and Windy's leash to Ushie.

6

After that, my days were split up between home, where I went when I had to, Ushie's, where I went as much as she wanted me, and Orland's, where I knew I was always welcome, if only for my work.

Orland was all excited that next week, running Golden Earrings every day and timing her, and talking about winning the Maiden Stakes at East St. Louis. It was a two-thousand-dollar purse, and he was pretty sure she could win it. He was also taking Wonderdog and Wallbanger for some puppy races.

A couple of days before Orland left for the races, he came over to where I was raking up dog chunks in one of the exercise yards. "Hey, Marty."

I quit raking and went over to the fence.

"Listen, Mack just called. He's got a run, out to the West Coast, and he ain't going to be able to watch the place for me while I'm gone. Think you're up to the job?"

Mack was Orland's brother-in-law, who usually came out and took care of the kennel while Orland was off on racing trips. But lately he'd been getting fairly steady work driving refrigerator trucks for a rabbit-packing plant outside Springfield.

I grinned. "Sure. How much will you pay me?"

He looked me up and down. "Five bucks a day."

It wasn't much, but I'd only be doing about the same stuff I was already doing for free. And he'd be gone eight days. That was forty dollars. I needed the money because I was buying Windy's dog food, and not the cheap stuff from the mill, either. Ushie kept saying she could afford it, and maybe she could, but Windy was still my dog and I wanted her food to be coming from me.

"Can I stay in your house while you're gone, like Mack?"

Orland looked down at me and squinted till his eyes disappeared behind his cheeks. "I don't care. You don't have to, but you can if you want, I guess."

He wandered off, scratching himself, and I went back to raking with a daydream growing in my mind. Eight whole days, living out here all by myself, with Windy living in the house with me. Perfect. Perfect!

About four I finished up, hosed off my filthy legs and arms with the hose at the side of the kennel, and coasted my bike down the highway toward downtown. The Divine Word Book and Bible Store was one of the few live stores left in town, it and the IGA on the corner, the plumbing and hardware store, and the two bars. There was also a café and a Country Crafts store that sold dolls made out of cornhusks, and stuff that was supposed to be antiques but looked like junk to me.

Mom was in her usual chair behind the counter, so low you couldn't see her till you were almost on top of her.

She'd had her feet up and was dozing with an opened book across her lap.

It was a narrow store, and dark. On the walls were pictures of Jesus, and little plaster figures of Him hanging on the cross. On the shelves were Bibles and other books that Mom called inspirational. There were a few greeting cards, and some paperback books that were supposed to be stories but actually just taught lessons, like the stories we used to have to read in the Sunday School papers. You'd start out thinking it was going to be a good story, and all it ended up being was another lesson. Why you shouldn't lie, or steal, or whatever. Why it's better to love than to hate. It used to make me so mad I quit reading those stories.

It was depressing to realize they had those same stories for adults. You'd think people that old wouldn't still need fake stories to tell them how to run their lives.

Mom woke up and dropped her feet to the floor when I came in. She looked at the clock, saw it was still half an hour till closing time, and sagged back.

"Mom, Orland needs me to take care of the kennels for him when he goes to East St. Louis next week. He'll pay me five dollars a day, okay?"

"Fine," she said, yawning.

"He wants me to stay out there at night, just to be sure the dogs are okay—you know, if a wolf or a badger or something like that would come around, or if a dog would get sick in the night. Okay?"

"Stay out there, all night? Alone?" She looked doubtful. "I don't think we could let you do that."

"Why?" I whined. "Nothing would happen to me. It's safe."

I knew from television that, these days, most places weren't safe for young girls out alone at night, but I'd never heard of anything happening to anyone in Jackson Ridge, just sometimes guys getting drunk in one of the bars and fighting, or a bunch of high-school kids knocking over rural mailboxes for devilment.

I was warming up for a strong argument when the door opened behind me and the floor shook with heavy steps.

"Well, if it isn't young Martha."

Stupid thing to say. I forced a smile and turned to face Brother George.

It was probably a serious sin to hate a minister, but I did, anyway. He was a huge man, loud and energetic and handsome, with a ton of black, curly hair and rosy cheeks and, worse yet, rosy lips. How could anyone trust a man with such red lips?

"Hello, George," Mom said in that funny soft voice. She stood up and leaned against the counter, like she wanted to get closer to him. I backed away a couple of steps.

Without taking her eyes off him, Mom said, "Marty, you best run on home now. I'll be along in a little bit."

I opened my mouth to protest. We were in the middle of something important here, the question of me staying alone at night out at Orland's, which would mean getting to have Windy with me for eight straight days, day and night, sleeping on my bed and everything. It was important!

But Mom looked at me and said, "Take a package of that hamburger out of the freezer and put it in the oven to thaw. Set it at three hundred. Go on now."

I went, but not home. I went to the corner of the building and then sort of eased back till I could see in the window, just at the edge. I don't know what made me do it, or what I thought I was going to see.

What I saw was nothing. They were both out of sight.

The store had a small back room, just a junky little storage place. The only way I could get to that window, though, was to go all the way to the end of the block and come back up the alley. I swung my bike around and went for it. Up the alley I rode, past the backs of all the old store buildings, past the rows of trash barrels and Dumpsters, to the familiar plank rear of the Divine Word Book and Bible Store.

I rode up right under the back window and stood up on my pedals to look in.

They were kissing.

Brother George had his arms, his whole self, wrapped around Mom, and she was wrapped around him, right back. I couldn't believe it.

Not that preacher.

Not my mom.

I fled, to Windy and to Ushie, but Ushie didn't have time to talk. It was her recital night, and she had to finish dusting and moving furniture.

With Windy shadowing me, I helped set out the chairs in Ushie's back parlor and did what dusting she'd trust me with. Her house had the two small square rooms that she called the front and back parlors, but they were really living room and dining room. The seven-foot George Steck grand piano took up the whole living room except for glass-fronted cases of sheet music and knickknack shelves of little glass animals and feather flowers.

The back parlor, on recital nights, held four rows of four chairs each, chairs she borrowed from the funeral parlor. The walls in there were crammed with musicale posters and programs, and more knickknacks till I didn't think we'd ever get them all dusted.

I wanted so bad to talk to her about George and Mom, but I knew she was thinking about her students and whether they'd do well enough, tonight, for their parents to keep sending them, and their five dollars, for lessons.

Ushie did let me open a couple of cans of soup and make supper for us while she went and changed into her black recital dress with the yellow lace collar. She wore a huge flowered handkerchief pinned on the front, and all her jewelry, three necklaces and a whole bunch of bracelets and rings.

When people started coming, I took Windsong out the back way and played with her in the yard. I tried to throw sticks and have her chase them, but she didn't understand. She seemed to want to run with me, but it was too hot and I was too depressed. I just lay down in the grass in the middle of the yard and let her run in big circles around me, while the music came floating out the back window.

There were seven students. When I'd counted seven songs I thought it was over, but it kept going on. They were playing more than one song each. It took forever.

I'd called home earlier and told Matt I was having supper with Ushie and helping with her recital, so I was free from home for a few hours, but still I wished everybody would hurry up and leave. I wanted Ushie to myself. With Orland gone, she was the only person I could, safely, tell.

When the music finally got over with, they still didn't leave. There were the little cookies and glasses of punch, and all the standing around talking about how much better Jessica was getting with her pedal work and what a shame it was that Kevin froze up just when he was doing so well.

Finally, finally, they all went home, and Ushie brought the leftover cookies and punch out to the back patio. Windy ran to her. I hated that, but told myself it was only for the cookies.

"It sounded good," I said, thinking I should say something about the recital.

"Yah, pretty good this time. I don't think I lose any students, yet a while."

"Ushie, something happened today, and I really need to talk to somebody about it."

She peered at me through the dark. "That why you been hanging around all night? You should've said something before."

"No, it's just, well, this afternoon I saw . . . my mom . . . kissing a man."

"Not your father."

I shook my head and offered Windy a piece of cookie.

"Who?"

I hesitated. This was scary. It was dangerous information to turn loose of.

She said, "Was it that George fellow?"

"Yes. How did you know?" I stared at her.

She shrugged. "He been going in that store a lot. And he's the type."

I stared harder. "But he's a minister, Ushie! Ministers don't do things like that. My mom is married, and so is he. How can a minister do something . . ."

She shoved back in her chair and toed out of her dressy black shoes. With a ring-laden hand she unbuttoned the top of her dress and folded it open to the night breeze.

"First place, he's not all that much of a minister, not a real one. He's got his little congregation out there in that garage-place. They call it a tabernacle; that don't make it one. And that radio program of his, that "Ministry of the Air." You don't have to be a genuine ordained minister of no real church to have a gospel show on a little no-account local radio station. All you have to do is have some money or some pull with the station manager."

I sat forward. "You mean he's not really a minister? He's always going around God-blessing everybody and putting his big old hand on people's heads like he was God touching them."

Yah, and there's plenty of foolish women that'll fall for a man like that just because he's paying them a little attention."

"But, my mom . . ."

"Your mother works for him, Marty."

"She what?" My jaw dropped again.

Ushie nodded. "He owns that Bible store and about half the buildings on that side of the block. He's got big plans, I guess. Going to be another Jim Bakker or Oral Roberts or some such. You know what he was before he got religion? He was selling rip-off building lots down on

White Lake, and he got closed down for illegal advertising. And before that he was running some kind of chain letter scheme out of Florida."

My eyes widened. "How do you know all this stuff, Ushie? You never go anyplace."

"People come here. My students' mothers, they love to carry a good story."

I got scared again then. "Don't tell anybody about Mom, will you? I have to figure out what to do about it, and I don't want anybody else to know."

"Take some punch. Finish it off. You don't need to do nothing about your mother, Marty. It's her business; leave her to it."

But pedaling home, I thought, it was my business, too.

Because if I told Daddy, he might get a divorce. And if he did that, he'd take Matt with him.

And then, Windy could come home.

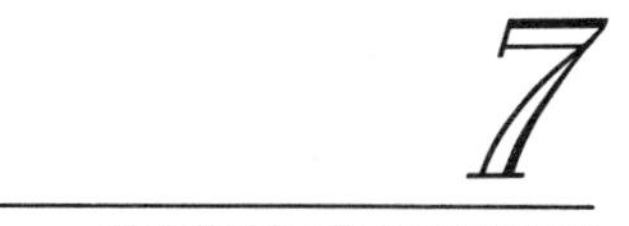

7

Orland left for East St. Louis, for six days of racing, and I put everything else on hold while I concentrated on taking care of the kennels. Daddy refused to let me stay up there overnight. He said it wasn't safe. I got so mad at him, I almost told him about Mom right then and there, but I held back. That still needed more thinking.

The first day of my job, I went by way of Ushie's and got Windy to take up there with me. Ushie wasn't awake yet, and it made her a little crabby when I knocked on the door, so I got out of there as fast as I could, with Windy running along beside my bike, through town and up the hill toward Orland's.

It was a cool blue morning, wet tasting and exciting. I just let Windy run loose around the place while I let dogs out into their exercise yards and started hauling feed and cleaning water buckets. I loved being there alone, being in charge of everything. As much as I liked Orland, I liked being here alone even better. I could pretend it was my place and my dogs, and I was grown up and safe.

Windsong lay in the shade with her head up and forelegs crossed daintily, watching me work. She looked like visiting royalty, and she probably felt that way, too, after her soft life at Ushie's.

When all the work was done, I went through the kennel and stared at one dog after another, trying to decide who I would breed Windy to, when she was old enough. I was pretty sure Orland would give me a free stud service, for all the work I did around the place. Then I'd have my own litter of greyhounds, some to sell, some to race.

The dream grew and grew in my head.

Which dog? There was Blackbeard the Pirate, sire of Prize Is Gold. Prize was Windsong's sire and grandsire, which would make Blackbeard a strong linebreeding combination with Windy. Blackbeard had been a good dog in his day and had sired some good ones.

Or there was Crossbones, a big yellow-brindle dog I'd never liked much because of his yellowish eyes and unfriendly attitude. He was faster than old Blackbeard had been, but he was bad about fighting other dogs.

Or there was Roll of Thunder, a red-and-white dog who wasn't very big, but he was fast and never gave up in a race. He had courage, Orland said, so he might be the one. . . .

I took Windy out to the practice track and started weeding. A lot of weeds were growing up through the sawdust on the inside part of the track, right where they could slow down the dogs if they got much bigger. Pretending the place was mine, I saw all kinds of things I wanted to improve. Windsong was nervous at first, remembering her terror in the starting box, but after a while she relaxed and moved around me, sniffing and circling.

It was a perfect day. I hated to leave at five, and to have to take Windy back to Ushie's. It was unnatural. We belonged together.

After supper Jodie asked me if I wanted to go to the mall in Springfield with her family. I went, just to get out of my house.

Next morning I had to wake Ushie up again, to get Windy. When she came to the door she looked crabbier than I've ever seen her.

"Just came to get Windy," I said as cheerily as I could.

"Well go away. You can't have her."

"What?" I stared, gape mouthed.

"You heard me. What makes you think you can come banging on my door, six o'clock in the morning, and take my dog off all day, just because you want to."

I just stared. Ushie was my friend!

"You know what your trouble is?" Ushie went on. "You're just plain selfish. You and all you kids. I'm sick and tired of you, always thinking about yourselves, what you want, never mind what anybody else wants. Never mind if I like this dog myself, never mind if I get lonesome now, if she's gone all day. You give her to me because you got to find a home for her, okay. So I take her. Then you act like I'm just a convenience, just someplace to dump your dog when it's convenient for you, and you can still come and take her off with you when it suits you."

The door shut in my face.

I could hear the tick of Windy's toenails on the floor inside as Ushie went back toward her bedroom.

I got through the morning chores with my head in a cloud of hate and confusion. When I nearly turned Crossbones out in the same exercise yard as Roll of Thunder, I woke up and started paying attention to what I was doing. Crossbones would have killed Thunder, and it would have been my fault.

Everything Ushie said to me played over and over through my head. It made me furious, and ashamed, and furious again. Selfish! All I was trying to do was save Windy's life and be with her as much as I could. What was so selfish about that?

But little cracks of logic broke through my fury, like sunlight through the fort's walls. From Ushie's viewpoint, it was possible that things might look the way she said. I hadn't thought about her, or her feelings about Windy. It hadn't occurred to me that an adult might need a dog the same way I did.

My mind was locked in to the idea that there was something special between Windy and me, and I clung to that idea. It seemed to justify everything. And I needed it to be true.

So . . . maybe Ushie might be a little bit right in thinking I was selfish. It didn't seem like selfishness to me; it just seemed like rightness and survival. But maybe to her . . .

Or maybe she was just crabby because I woke her up so early.

In any case, it shook me up. I started thinking, if I really was a selfish person, maybe that was why Mom and Daddy preferred Matt. Maybe all my problems really were my own fault, and not everybody else's.

I cleaned the kennel and brushed down all the dogs to make them feel good. I made lunch from bread and baloney in Orland's kitchen, then spent the afternoon trying to understand a book called *Canine Genetics, Their Practical Application*.

But I couldn't concentrate. The book was too hard, and I couldn't get my mind off Ushie, and Windy, and the revelation that I might not be a nice person.

The next day I didn't go to Ushie's at all. I hoped she was feeling awful for what she'd said to me, but I knew she probably wasn't. She was probably enjoying Windy and enjoying not having me hanging around. I hated that thought.

In the afternoon, when the work was done and I was just rolling up empty dog food bags and stuffing them inside other empty dog food bags to try to make the place look neater, Jodie came up. She'd never been there before, so it surprised me.

I showed her around the place, then we sat on the back porch with cans of pop from Orland's refrigerator. She talked about her stuff awhile, about Raye's boyfriend and all the uproar he was causing in Raye's family, and how Roger really was a nice guy if you got to know him.

I didn't care about any of it. Maybe I *was* selfish. I listened till she ran down, but I didn't care about Raye or Roger or any of it. Windy was the only important thing.

I had to get her back. That was the whole game, right there. I had to somehow get Windy back before Ushie got so attached to her that I'd never get her back.

The pain at the bottom of the pain was that Windy might already be getting as attached to Ushie as she was to me. I couldn't stand that thought.

When Jodie's talk ran down, I said, "Jodie, if a family gets divorced, do the kids get to choose who they want to live with?"

Jodie shrugged. "I guess. Well, I guess they get to have a vote in it, but probably the parents really decide, you know, who gets the kids and the house and all that. I think the mother usually gets to keep the kids. When my Aunt Cindy got divorced, her husband tried to take the kids, and he didn't get them.

"Why?" she asked as an afterthought.

"Just wondering. Sometimes I wonder what would happen if my mom and dad get divorced."

"Your dad would keep Matt, I bet."

I nodded.

"Your mom might get to keep you, though, especially if your dad got Matt."

"I'd be the consolation prize, you mean?"

"No." She punched my leg. "But I bet that's what would happen. Your dad would never give up Matt."

"Maybe Mom wouldn't give him up, either."

Jodie shrugged. "It would depend on whose fault the divorce was, too. I mean, if your dad was the unfaithful one and your mom caught him with some other woman, she could probably get to keep both you and Matt if she wanted to."

I breathed more faintly. "What if she was the unfaithful one? What if my dad caught her with another man?"

"Then he could keep whatever kids he wanted, I guess."

"He'd keep Matt."

It was beginning to fall into place in my mind.

Orland came home five days later. I was at his place when he drove in, and I could see his fat, grinning face even before he got out of his pickup.

He grabbed me in a crushing hug; he'd never done that before.

"We done good," he bellowed. "Wonderdog won all three of his races, and Golden Earrings came in second in a strong field in the big Maiden Stakes, and she won a smaller race the last day of the meet. And I sold Wallbanger for forty-five hundred dollars."

He did a quick check of the kennels to be sure everybody was still okay. Then, grinning like a fool, he handed me a one-hundred-dollar bill instead of the forty he actually owed me.

"I made a total profit," he said expansively, "of thirteen thousand eight hundred dollars. That's after all the motels and meals and entries. I feel like this business is finally getting off the ground, Marty. It's been my dream all my life, and now it's finally coming together. That Golden Earrings bitch, she's the key, she's the best I've had, and

Wonderdog is going to be even better. I hope you'll stay available for taking care of the kennel, because I'm hitting the road just as fast as I can get entries in. Going up to Omaha, and over through Waterloo and Dubuque for their seasons, back down through Illinois and Arkansas, that'll take most of July and all of August and September, and after that, come back, take a breather, then head down to Mississippi and Louisiana for the winter circuits. By that time I'll be so rich I can afford a full-time kennel man."

That scared me.

He saw it in my eyes. "Aw, don't worry, rat-faced kid. You'll still be my top hand. Heck, by the time you get out of high school I'll be ready to take you on as a paid assistant trainer. How's your bitch?"

I couldn't answer.

He looked at me again. We were standing over the gate to the biggest exercise yard, watching Wonderdog and Golden Earrings stretch their legs after a week of kenneling and traveling.

"I said, how's your bitch?"

"I had to give her away. Sort of. I couldn't keep her at home, they just plain wouldn't let me. And I knew if I brought her back here, you'd put her down. So I took her over to my old piano teacher's. Mrs. Fretty. I just meant to leave her there till I could figure out something better, but now she's gotten so attached to Windy, I don't think she even wants me to come over there anymore."

"Ah. Well, that sounds okay, doesn't it? The dog's got a good home, that's the main thing."

No, I wanted to shout. The main thing was that I loved

Windsong, and missed her, and wanted to be with her.

"Orland?"

"What?" He was walking around now, kicking the ground and staring at the kennel building.

"Would you give me Windsong's registration papers? So she'd be legally mine?"

"I guess. If you want them. But if you already gave the dog away, why would you want the papers?"

He was staring at the kennel, hardly listening to me.

"Orland?"

"What?"

"If I could figure out a way of getting Windsong back and keeping her, would you let me breed her to one of your dogs next year? So I could have my own litter, and maybe race one of them?"

He looked down at me. "Might. Well, heck, all the money I'll be paying you to take care of the place while I'm off on these racing circuits, you can afford to pay stud fees, same as anybody else. What I'm thinking, I could build on, out this direction, or I could add another twenty feet on at the other end. Or, I could start a whole new building over on that flat part over there. What do you think?"

I tried to get excited with him about expanding the kennels, but all I could think of was getting Windy back and making my own dreams come true.

That night I lay awake in the dark, listening for Mom's car to come in. Her and Daddy had sniped at each other all through supper, and she took off without a word of explanation as soon as the dishes were done.

Around ten-thirty, her car coasted up beside the house. I was out of bed and downstairs on the screen porch by the time she came through the door.

"Mom?"

"Marty? Is that you? Lord, child, you scared me out of a year's growth. What are you doing setting out here in the dark?"

"Just thinking, and waiting for you. I wanted to talk to you."

She sighed. "Can it wait till morning? I'm not feeling too good, hon."

I didn't say anything.

She sighed again and came to sit on the glider beside me. She put her arm around me and pulled me against her shoulder, and pushed us off into rocking motion with her toe.

"Mom?"

"What."

"If you and Daddy got divorced . . ."

She sat up abruptly. "Where'd you ever get that notion?"

"Well, y'all are always sniping at one another. . . ."

"That don't mean we don't love each other," she said firmly.

"Do you?"

"What, love each other? Of course we do. Think we'd of stayed married all these years if we didn't?"

"Well, if you did decide to get a divorce, who would us kids live with?"

She slowed the rocking and got very quiet. "Who would you want to live with?" she asked finally, as though the words were being dragged out of her.

"I'd want to live with you. Definitely. And Matt would want to live with Daddy."

She sat away from me and stared at me through the dark. "You've talked about this with Matt?"

"No. I haven't talked about it with anybody, but he's just such a daddy's boy. They always want to be together. He'd choose Daddy, if he got to choose. And I'd choose you."

"Thank you, darlin' " she said faintly.

We rocked and listened to the night birds and insects and the roar of somebody's pipes down on the highway.

"Mom?"

"I'm afraid to ask, what?"

"If it did work out that way, if you and Daddy got a divorce and Daddy moved out and took Matt, and it was just you and me living together . . ."

"Yes?"

"Could I have Windy back?"

Her breath came out in a long whoosh. "Is that what all this is about? That dog? I thought she was getting along fine at Ushie's."

"She is, but I miss her so much, Mom. Ushie said I was selfish, she said I just dumped Windy on her for my own convenience, and then I was always taking Windy away when Ushie wanted her for company. So I don't feel like I can even go over there to visit Windy anymore, and I can't stand it."

"So . . . What? So you're hoping your parents will get a divorce so you can have your dog back? Good Lord, Marty."

When she said it that way, it did sound awful.

I got up, sighing. "Forget it. I was just, well, it's scary when your parents fight and you think they might break up, and you don't know what's going to happen, where you'd end up. It's scary."

She stood up then, too, and pulled me in for a long, warm hug. Combing my hair back from my face with her fingers, she said, "Well, it's not likely to happen, but if it does, I can assure you I would keep you with me."

"What about Matt?"

"I don't know. Depending on the circumstances, I might be forced to give him up to his daddy, but I'd try to keep him, too."

Back in my bed, I stared up at the sloping ceiling for hours and tried to sort it out.

If they got a divorce, Mom would definitely keep me. That made me feel wonderful.

But, she said she'd also try to keep Matt. But her voice was different when she'd said that, much less sure. It sounded as though she might be saying what a mother is supposed to say, that she'd try to keep both her children, but yet at the same time, like she knew she might not be able to keep Matt.

She knew she was guilty, that was the whole thing. She knew she was sneaking around to see Brother George. Naturally she didn't know I knew about it, but she sure as heck knew, and that was why she'd sounded unsure about keeping Matt.

If Daddy knew about Brother George, he could get the

divorce on his own terms, and that would mean keeping Matt. He wouldn't want to be bothered with me; he'd let Mom have me, but he'd never let her have Matt.

And that was exactly what I was counting on.

Tell Daddy about Brother George.

Wait for the divorce to go through, and Daddy and Matt to move out.

Then, with Windy's registration papers from Orland, to prove she was mine legally, I'd go to Ushie and explain, and she'd have to give Windy back.

I fell asleep almost smiling.

9

The Divine Word Tabernacle used to be a garage and used-car lot, on the north edge of town, where the mountainside came right down to the highway. It stood on a level place scooped out from the hillside, with a big parking lot to one side.

The building itself was cinder block painted cream, with long, jagged cracks zigzagging among the blocks. One whole corner of the building bulged at the bottom. It had big windows all across the front, from when it was a car showroom.

From my hiding place in the woods I could see every detail in that lighted building, just like it was a stage. Wednesday night gospel services.

There were maybe twenty people inside, mostly old people with nothing else to do. Mom was there, in a front row over toward the side. Jodie and her family were in there, too, the kids squirming and poking at one another, cousin Raye staring holes in the back of Roger's head. They might be starting the evening with their families, but they'd end up by taking off together.

Up in front, of course, was Brother George, looking dramatic and handsome and powerful in his long, black robe with gold satin draped around his neck.

The doors and windows were open for air, and I could hear his voice pounding on, not the words, but that big sure voice just like it sounded on the radio. He always talked like God was his best friend, like he was passing on important messages from his friend God to the rest of us ordinary people.

I hated that. I didn't figure he knew God any more than I did, it was just all a big fake. Nobody really had the right to speak for God, especially not a man who would mess around with a married woman with two children. Where did he get off, acting so pure and noble while he was doing that?

I wanted to hurt him. Him, and Daddy and Matt. I didn't want to hurt Mom, but I couldn't see any way around that. Still, this whole thing was her decision, getting involved with Brother George in the first place.

Tonight was going to be the night.

The service was over by nine. It took another half hour for everybody to have their turn to talk to Brother George and shake his hand and all that. Then, finally, only Mom and George were left inside, and the lights went out.

I scrambled down the hill to where I'd hid my bike and peeled out of there. It was a seven-minute ride home, pumping as hard as I could even on the downhill parts.

Matt was alone in the living room, watching TV.

"Where's Daddy?" My voice sounded quavery, but he didn't notice. He just pointed toward the bedroom behind the living room.

Timidly, I pushed the door open.

Daddy was sitting on the edge of the bed, crying.

His hands, hanging down between his knees, were holding a silver picture frame. I knew the picture. It was their wedding picture, the two of them standing in the wind and the sun, on the steps of the church. Mom's hair and veil were blowing up around her face; she looked beautiful.

He wasn't sobbing out loud, he just sat there staring bleakly out the back window, with tears on his face.

He didn't hear me.

I stood there staring at him.

Canned laughter came from the TV, from some silly program Matt was watching about a family that has a series of problems but they really love each other and everything always works out for them, with love and understanding and everyone hugging in the last scene.

But it wasn't that way in real life.

Daddy was hurting, and it wasn't going to go away.

He already knew what I'd been about to tell him. He might not have known exactly where Mom was at that instant, but he knew she was interested in another man. If I went to him right then and told him what I'd seen, chances are, he would feel like he had to do something. Say something. Make a big deal out of it.

And probably they would get a divorce. And probably I'd get Windy, in the end.

But my daddy was hurting, so bad. I never even thought about that. And if they got a divorce, my mom would be hurt awful bad, too. George wouldn't leave his wife and take up with Mom, and if he did, he'd just be unfaithful to her like he was being now to his wife. Mom wouldn't ever be happy with George, but maybe if this thing didn't get dragged out and talked about and forced, maybe it would blow over and Mom and Daddy would fix it up between them, someway.

All this went through my head in about a second, while I stood in that doorway seeing my daddy's pain for the first time.

I wanted to go and hug him and make him feel better, but I couldn't. Him and me, we just never got in that habit. So I did the one thing I could do.

I backed out of the room and closed the door.

10

I found Orland in the workroom of the kennel. Crossbones was standing on the low-built grooming table, his yellow eyes glittering with hate, his lips curled inside the muzzle he wore. Orland was sitting on the short-legged stool he used when he worked on the dogs' feet.

Orland wasn't fussy about much, but he did take awful good care of his dogs' nails and feet. If a greyhound's toenails grew long enough to touch the ground it could make their feet spread out, weakening them so they couldn't run at their full speed. He had a nail grinder that looked like an electric drill, but with a round stone wheel that spun so fast you couldn't see it, and he sanded off the tips of the dogs' toenails. Most of the dogs got used to it while they were still puppies, but old Crossbones never did give in to it. He was too mean.

I started to decide not ever to breed Windy to him. Then my black cloud came down over me, like it had been all night since I saw Daddy holding that picture. I needed . . . something . . . this morning. Awful bad.

What I needed was my dog to cry on, but Orland was the next best thing.

I took my usual seat, on the pile of dog food bags in the corner near Orland. He glanced over at me as he shifted himself and his stool around to Crossbones's hind foot.

"You look like you been drug through the hedge backward," he commented cheerfully.

"Thanks."

He ground down all four toenails, *bzzz*, *bzzz*, *bzzz*, *bzzz*, then shifted around to the other hind foot. Finally he stood up and started feeling around Crossbones's neck, just behind an ear.

"What?" I said

"Little lump under the skin. It's unattached; can't be anything serious."

Just his orneriness coming out, probably."

"I reckon." He released the dog's head from the holding noose, unbuckled the muzzle, and turned Crossbones loose. First thing the dog did when he hit the floor was lift his leg against the side of Orland's pants, his charming way of getting even for the nail trim. He did it every time.

I walked along with Orland, taking Crossbones back to his run. "How come you let him do that to you, every time?" I asked. He put the dog away and stopped by the hose to run a stream of water over the wet streak on his jeans. It was a hot morning and he was wearing ratty old canvas shoes, so I figured the hose water felt good to him.

"Only fair," he grunted.

There was a place under a shade tree where a person could sit and watch all the dogs in all the runs and pens, down the whole length of the kennel. Orland had an old bench-type car seat there, braced up against the tree. I think it was out of an old wrecked pickup truck out in the weeds. If you watched out for the scratchy places where the plastic upholstery was ripped, it made a great place to sit and watch the dogs.

Or talk.

"What's eating you, this morning?" he said, lowering his bulky body down to the car seat.

First I was going to say, "Nothing," but he knew better, and besides, I really wanted to talk it all out with somebody who had good sense. Orland had the best sense of anybody I knew.

"If I tell you something, you won't tell anybody, will you?"

He looked at me like it was an insult that I even asked.

"Well," I said slowly, "I almost did something last night, and I think it would have been a really awful thing to do, but it might have gotten me Windy back from Ushie, or it might not have, and now I half hate myself for even thinking about doing it, and half hate myself for not going through with it and maybe getting Windy."

"That's clear as mud," he snorted. He looked down over his fat cheeks at me, waiting to hear the rest of it.

"You're probably too busy, this morning," I said, because I needed to know he cared enough about me to take the time to listen.

"Toenails can wait," he said.

From him, that was pretty good. That ranked me pretty high. I relaxed a little, and it all started spilling out, about seeing Mom and Brother George together, and what Jodie had said about divorced parents dividing up the kids, and what Mom said about keeping me but maybe not Matt, and how scared I was that Windy was getting to love Ushie more than me. And about what I almost did last night, telling Daddy that Mom was with George right then, egging him on to leaving her. All so I could get Windy back.

He sat for a long time, staring out over the pens of dogs. There wasn't much to look at. Mostly they were just lying in the shallow dust holes they'd dug for themselves to keep cool in. A pair of pups were wrestling and chewing on each other's throats, but halfheartedly, as though it was too hot even for that.

I began to get scared at how long it was taking him to say anything.

"You're starting to grow up," Orland said finally. There was approval in his voice. It was the last thing I expected. Disgust was more like what I expected.

"How do you mean?"

"I mean," he explained, "when you saw your daddy like that you could feel his hurt, and it was bigger than your own, and you knew it. That's growing up, kid, in case you didn't know it."

"What do you mean?" I kind of knew, but I wanted him to go on.

"Just, you were in a situation where you could have hurt a lot of other people, for your own selfish purpose, and you didn't do it. That makes you a good, mature person, don't matter how old you are."

"Was I being selfish before?"

"Yeah, probably. All kids start out selfish; can't help

it. Kids got no power of their own, so they have to get what they need any way they can. A baby's hungry; it cries till someone feeds it. Nobody calls that selfish; it's just surviving. You got needs, too. You need dogs. Lots of people need dogs and can't have them, one reason or another. You'll have your dogs, Marty. Just a matter of time, and you'll have your dogs, but now is when you need them. I know that."

My throat was lumping up.

He went on, his voice soft now. "I know it because I needed dogs just like you, all the time I was growing up."

I looked at him, and suddenly I could see a fat little boy, lonesome and picked on by the other kids because of the way he looked. Bleeding inside, crying inside because there was nobody or nothing that loved him.

His voice got brisk, as if he was embarrassed, showing me that much about himself.

"So, let's look at the problem."

"The problem is I need Windy."

"What's the problem underneath that one? Think."

"I need dogs? I need something to love me? What do you mean?"

"I mean," he explained, "that maybe you need to be giving yourself a little support. That's what I had to learn to do, and it's what got me through life so far. Okay, look here. Look at facts. Your parents are separate people from you. Right? They've got their own problems that they're trying to rassle with, right now, and it's problems that don't have anything to do with you. They have to either straighten out their marriage or end it, one or the other, but it hasn't got anything to do with you. So what you have to do is back off from them and start working on building your own strength, away from them."

"What about Matt?"

"Matt's got his own problems, and he'll probably have a whole lot more as he grows older. You say he's the favored child in the family. I got news for you. That ain't no favor they're doing him. He's learning some lessons that are false, is what's happening to him right now. He's learning that he can manipulate his mom and daddy and get what he wants out of them, but that ain't going to hold, once he gets out in the real world. That's when everything's going to come unraveled for that boy. In the end, you'll be the lucky one of the two, because you got toughened up to life, and you learned to be your own provider, if you follow me."

"No."

"Okay, let me put it this way. You want dogs? Then you make it happen, for yourself. Don't go depending on dirty tricks to get what you want from other people, get it for yourself, straight arrow."

I liked what he was saying. "How? How do I get it for myself, straight arrow?"

"You know how. You use your head and your energy, and you use what you've got at hand. What's that? Think."

Glumly I said, "I've got the fact that I'm only thirteen. Not much I can do, at this age."

"Think again. What you've got is five, six years ahead of you before you're old enough to live on your own. Use that time to work, earn the money you'll need, learn what you need to learn, so you'll be ready when the time comes.

Set yourself goals, and stick to them. Do it for yourself, do you see what I'm getting at?"

I absorbed it for a while, then said, "But what about Windy?"

"Leave her be."

I stared at him, my throat lumping up again.

"Leave her be," he repeated. "She and Ushie are happy together, and when things settle down to normal, when Ushie knows for sure you're not going to try to take Windy away from her, you can visit her over there, I bet. But you'd be better off spending your time up here, learning greyhounds with me, if racing dogs is what you want to do with your life."

"Forget Windy?" I fought back the tears.

"No, just let go of her and move on. And remember her for what she gave you."

"What?" I whispered.

"Heck, girl, she gave you more than your folks ever gave Matt. She showed you how to care about other people."

I stared off through the dust cloud the pups were raising in the shafts of morning sun. Orland was right. I could feel it all the way through me.

His truth wrapped around my heart and eased it, like prying stiff fingers off a tug-of-war rope. In that moment I gave Windy and Ushie to each other and, with a feeling of gathering strength, I stood and pulled Orland up.

"Come on, boss, let's go grind toenails."